# EDDYCAT
## Attends Sunshine's Birthday Party

For a free color catalog describing Gareth Stevens's list of high-quality children's books, call 1-800-341-3569 (USA) or 1-800-461-9120 (Canada).

Library of Congress Cataloging-in-Publication Data

Barnett, Ada.
    Eddycat attends Sunshine's birthday party / by Ada Barnett, Pam Manquen, and Linda Rapaport ; illustrated by Mark Hoffmann.
       p. cm. -- (Social skill builders for children)
    Includes bibliographical references and index.
    Summary: Buddy shows how to behave properly while attending Sunshine's birthday party. At various intervals in the story, Eddycat makes additional comments about party etiquette.
       ISBN 0-8368-0943-2
    [1. Parties--Fiction. 2. Etiquette--Fiction. 3. Birthdays--Fiction. 4. Animals--Fiction.] I. Manquen, Pam. II. Rapaport, Linda. III. Hoffmann, Mark, ill. IV. Series.
PZ7.B2629Ec   1993
[E]--dc20                                                                                   92-56881

Published by
**Gareth Stevens Publishing**
1555 North RiverCenter Drive, Suite 201
Milwaukee, Wisconsin  53212, USA

This edition of *Eddycat Attends Sunshine's Birthday Party* was first published in the USA and Canada by Gareth Stevens, Inc., in association with The Children's Etiquette Institute.  Text, artwork, characters, design, and format © 1993 by The Children's Etiquette Institute.

Sincere thanks to educators Jody Henderson-Sykes of Grand Avenue Middle School in Milwaukee, Wisconsin, and Mel Ciena of the University of San Francisco for their invaluable help.

EDDYCAT, EddieCat, and the EDDYCAT symbol and Social Skills for Children are trademarks and service marks of the American Etiquette Institute.

Printed in the United States of America

1 2 3 4 5 6 7 8 9 98 97 96 95 94 93

Children's Etiquette Institute
Social Skill Builders for Children
EDDYCAT

# EDDYCAT
## Attends Sunshine's Birthday Party

Gareth Stevens Publishing
**MILWAUKEE**

# CONTENTS

Introduction. . . . . . . . . . . . . . . . . . . . . . . . . . . . . . . 5

*Eddycat Attends Sunshine's Birthday Party* . . . . . . . . . . . . 6

Eddycat's Helpful Terms. . . . . . . . . . . . . . . . . . . . . 29

More Books to Read . . . . . . . . . . . . . . . . . . . . . . . . 30

Place to Write . . . . . . . . . . . . . . . . . . . . . . . . . . . . 30

Parent/Teacher Guide. . . . . . . . . . . . . . . . . . . . . . . 31

Index. . . . . . . . . . . . . . . . . . . . . . . . . . . . . . . . . . 32

Hi, friends! Remember me? I'm Eddycat, and I live in a city named Mannersville.

Everyone here believes there is something special about certain words and sentences because they make others smile and feel good.

My goal is to try to make the world a better place in which to live, but I need your help. What you need to do is let others know that you care about them and that you care about yourself. I will show you the special way of doing this. And it will make me very happy to cheer you on as you learn to say the special words and follow the special rules!

Today, I am going to help Sunshine Smithbear be a wonderful hostess and a gracious guest of honor at her birthday party. In addition, Buddy Brownbear and the others will learn how to be wonderful guests. If you pay close attention, you will learn these things, too.

Here are some of the special phrases and magical words used in this Eddycat story. Can **you** find these words and sentences in the story?

| | |
|---|---|
| *Please.* | *May I?* |
| *Thank you.* | *No, thank you.* |
| *You're welcome.* | *I'm sorry.* |

Today is Sunshine's birthday.  She is excited
because her friends are coming to her party.
Her first guest has arrived!  It's Buddy Brownbear.

"Please come in, Buddy.  I'm so happy that you
could come to my party," says Sunshine.

"Hello, Sunshine.  Hello, Mr. and Mrs. Smithbear,"
says Buddy.

Buddy knows
that when he arrives at
Sunshine's house, it is important
for him to be polite and greet
Sunshine's parents, too.

After everyone arrives, the guests pick numbers for the pin-the-tail-on-the-donkey game.

"My number is four, so I will be fourth in line. I'll take my turn after you, Rhonda," says Buddy to Rhonda Rabbit.

After the game, it is time to eat.

"I found the place card with my name on it, so I know where Sunshine wants me to sit," says Harry Hound to Clara Duck.

"Happy birthday to you, happy birthday to you," sing Sunshine's guests.

"Thank you," says Buddy as he puts a piece of fruit on his plate.

When Mother Smithbear passes the ice cream cones, Buddy says, "No, thank you."

Buddy always takes small bites of food, and he does not wave his silverware around like Becky Bunny does.

When Seymour Smithbear accidentally spills his drink, he says, "I'm sorry."

Buddy uses his silverware to eat, but Buster
Bull is eating with his fingers! Which way do
you think is the correct way to eat ice cream
and cake?

It is not polite for Buster, or any other guest, to
lick his fingers.

Buddy never reaches in front of anyone. Instead, he says, "Please pass the fruit."

"Thank you," says Buddy.

Before Buddy takes a drink, he wipes his mouth with a napkin.  This way, he won't leave cake or other food on his glass.

Sunshine always waits to talk until her mouth is empty.  She also waits for the other person to finish talking before she begins to talk.

It is nice for all the guests to talk softly so that everyone can hear what is being said.  Also, food should be chewed quietly so as not to disturb others.

17

Did you notice how Buddy chews his food with his mouth closed?  Do you always remember to eat this way?

When not eating, Buddy keeps his hands folded in his lap – no elbows on the table, please.

18

"May I have more juice, please?" Sunshine asks her mother.

After Buddy finishes eating, he puts his silverware in the middle of his plate, like this. Mr. and Mrs. Smithbear know when he has finished because they see the silverware placed this way.

Because Buddy leaves his silverware on his plate like this, it won't fall off when Mr. and Mrs. Smithbear pick up his plate.

When you are ready to leave the table, put your napkin on the table, like this. Do not refold it!

Oh, boy! That's easy. I know how NOT to fold a napkin!

Everyone waits for Sunshine, the hostess, to
leave the table first.

Sunshine and her guests go into the living room where she opens her presents.

"Thank you, Buddy, for the pretty book about flowers," says Sunshine.

"You're welcome, Sunshine. I'm glad you like it," says Buddy, smiling.

"Good-bye, Harry. Thank you for coming to my party," says Sunshine.

"Good-bye, Mr. and Mrs. Smithbear. Good-bye, Sunshine. I had a very nice time at your party. Thank you for inviting me," says Becky as she hops down the steps.

"This is an extra gift for you, Sunshine, from your father and me," says Mother Smithbear.

"Now you have your own special 'thank you' cards to send to friends," says Father Smithbear.

"Thank you for coming to my party. I hope you had a wonderful time," says Sunshine to *you*!

Please join us in the next book when Buddy and Harry learn how to use the telephone. Would you like to learn, too?

I'm excited about learning how to use the telephone!

# EDDYCAT'S HELPFUL TERMS

**apologize**
To say you are sorry when you have made a mistake.

**consideration**
Thinking about another person's feelings and making sure not to do or say anything that would make someone feel uncomfortable or left out.

**etiquette**
The special rules for how to behave and treat others.

**invitation**
A card or letter inviting you to a party or other event.

**table manners**
Special rules for eating politely. Table manners include asking others to pass food to you rather than reaching across the table yourself, keeping your elbows off the table, and chewing with your mouth closed.

**"Thank you."**
A polite way to respond to someone who has done something nice or thoughtful for you.

**thank you card**
A card you send to someone in order to thank the person for something he or she has done for you.

**"You're welcome."**
A polite way to respond when someone thanks you.

# MORE BOOKS TO READ

The *Eddycat* series is the only truly authoritative collection on etiquette written for children. Nonetheless, the additional titles by other authors listed here represent good support for the concept that courtesy and manners are valuable skills and habits.

**Nonfiction:**
*Eddycat and Buddy Entertain a Guest.* Barnett, Manquen, Rapaport (Gareth Stevens)
*Eddycat Goes Shopping with Becky Bunny.* Barnett, Manquen, Rapaport (Gareth Stevens)
*Eddycat Helps Sunshine Plan Her Party.* Barnett, Manquen, Rapaport (Gareth Stevens)
*Eddycat Introduces. . . Mannersville.* Barnett, Manquen, Rapaport (Gareth Stevens)
*Eddycat Teaches Telephone Skills.* Barnett, Manquen, Rapaport (Gareth Stevens)

*The Muppet Guide to Magnificent Manners.* Howe (Random)
*My First Party Book.* Wilkes (Knopf)
*What Do You Say? A Child's Guide to Manners.* Snell (David and Charles)
*What to Do When Your Mom or Dad Says . . ."Be Kind to Your Guest."* Berry (Living Skills)
*Your Manners Are Showing.* Baker (Child's World)

**Fiction:**
*Dinner at Alberta's.* Hoban (Harper)
*Going to a Party.* Civardi and Cartwright (EDC)

# PLACE TO WRITE

For more information about etiquette, contact the American Etiquette Institute, P.O. Box 700508, San Jose, CA 95170.

# PARENT/TEACHER GUIDE

**conversation** page 17

Conversation is permitted and encouraged at the table. Guests should take small bites so that they are always ready to make a comment or answer a question.

**end of the meal** page 20

When a guest has finished eating, he or she should place the silverware diagonally across the center of the plate, parallel to each other. The fork tines should be up, and the spoon and/or knife should be in back of the fork, blade facing the fork. The host/hostess signals the end of the meal by placing his or her napkin on the table and rising.

**gifts/thank you cards** pages 22, 27

If a present or gift is given in person, the gift-giver should be thanked at the time. For gifts that are not delivered in person, the recipient should write a note on a card to acknowledge the gift and to thank the sender. The card should be handwritten and mention the gift specifically. It is always thoughtful and correct to send a thank you card for a gift, a favor, or any kindness shown to you.

**good-byes** pages 24, 25, 28

When a guest is ready to leave, it is her or his responsibility to find the host/hostess and thank him or her for the invitation. A very brief, "Good-bye, I had a wonderful time," is sufficient.

**greetings** page 6

For a children's party, the young host/hostess should stand at the door with the parents to greet the guests. Guests under the age of four should be instructed to say, "Happy birthday." Older children should know how to do a self introduction.

**napkin**                                        pages 9, 14, 16, 20

   The napkin is placed across your lap.  It is never tucked under a belt or under the chin, with the exception of very small children.  Always wipe your mouth with a napkin before drinking.  The napkin is left on the chair if you leave the table temporarily.  The napkin is left on the table only when the meal is completely over.  The napkin is never refolded.

**second helpings**

   It is not correct to ask for seconds unless the host/hostess has offered them.

**silverware**                                    pages 11, 12, 14, 20

   Once silverware is used, it is never returned to the table. While eating with a fork, do not hold the knife in the other hand. The knife is only held when cutting food.  It is not correct to heap food onto the back of the fork with a knife.

# INDEX

apologizing 13

elbows 18

food 10, 12, 14

games 7
gift-giving 21, 22, 27
greetings 6

napkins 9, 14, 16, 20

place cards 8
posture 8

silverware 11, 12, 14, 20

table manners 8-21
taking turns 7
thank you cards 27